For Max, who dove right in. - DMS

To my family who have made life anything but boring...
and a special thanks to Corie and James. - DK

First published in 2009 by Simply Read Books
www.simplyreadbooks.com

Text copyright©2009 David Michael Slater
Illustrations copyright©2009 Doug Keith

Library and Archives Canada Cataloguing in Publication

Slater, David Michael
    The bored book / David Michael Slater ; illustrations by Doug Keith.

ISBN 978-1-897476-19-2

    I. Keith, Doug II. Title.

PZ7.S62887Bo 2009   j813'.54   C2009-900910-2

Book Design by Pablo Mandel / CircularStudio.com

10 9 8 7 6 5 4 3 2 1

Printed in Singapore

THE BORED BOOK

David Michael Slater
Illustrations by Doug Keith

SIMPLY READ BOOKS